A ROOKIE BIOGRAPHY

L. FRANK BAUM

Author of

The Wonderful Wizard of Oz

By Carol Greene

 CHILDRENS PRESS®

CHICAGO

This book is for Diane Babb.

L. Frank Baum (1856-1919)

Library of Congress Cataloging-in-Publication Data

Greene, Carol.
    L. Frank Baum: author of the Wonderful Wizard of OZ / by Carol
Greene.
        p.   cm. — (A Rookie biography)
    Includes index.
    ISBN 0-516-04264-5
    1. Baum. L. Frank (Lyman Frank), 1856-1919—Juvenile literature.
2. Authors, American—20th century—Biography—Juvenile literature.
3. Oz (Imaginary place)—Juvenile literature. [1. Baum. L. Frank (Lyman
Frank), 1856-1919. 2. Authors, American.] I. Title. II. Series: Greene,
Carol. Rookie biography.
PS3503.A923Z67   1995   94-37514
                                                   CIP
                                                   AC

L. Frank Baum
was a real person.
He lived from 1856 to 1919.
Frank wrote many
books for children,
including *The Wonderful
Wizard of Oz.*
This is his story.

TABLE OF CONTENTS

Chapter 1   Scary Things and Secret
            Places   5
Chapter 2   From School to Axle Grease . . . 11
Chapter 3   Oz! 19
Chapter 4   More Oz 31
Chapter 5   Ozcot 37
Important Dates 46
Index 47

Chapter 1

Scary Things and
Secret Places

There it hung in the field,
big and spooky and still.
But wait! It moved!
It was getting down
from its post.

Its long, long legs
brought it closer, closer.
It was going to get him!

Little Frank Baum
woke up screaming.
He'd had the nightmare again,
the scarecrow nightmare.

"He reads too many fairy tales,"
said Frank's parents.
"And he's not very healthy."

Frank *did* love fairy tales
and he *wasn't* healthy.
He had angina pectoris,
a heart problem
that made his chest hurt.

A street in Syracuse, New York, as it looked when L. Frank Baum was born

But Frank still had fun
with his brothers and sisters.
They lived on a farm, Rose Lawn,
near Syracuse, New York.

The children played croquet,
baseball, and other games.
They had friends over
and went for carriage rides.

Frank's parents, Cynthia and Benjamin Baum

They didn't even have to leave
Rose Lawn to go to school.
Mr. and Mrs. Baum hired
teachers to come to them.

Frank couldn't play rough games
because of his heart.
But his mind got
plenty of exercise.

Frank liked to hide in
secret places with his toys
and make-believe friends.
There he made up stories.
He wanted to write
fairy tales someday.

But Frank knew how much
witches and goblins scared him.
So he promised himself
that he wouldn't put
scary things in *his* tales.

Frank didn't keep that promise.

Peekskill Academy (below) was located in
the beautiful Hudson River valley (above).

Chapter 2

From School to Axle Grease

When Frank was twelve,
his doctor said he could
go away to boarding school.
Frank's parents chose
Peekskill Academy
in Peekskill, New York.

Peekskill was a military school.
Boys there learned to march
and shoot a gun.
They played rough games.

Peekskill Academy as it looked in the 1930s

Frank hated it.
He hated always being busy.
He hated the way
teachers hit students.
He hated the rough games
and the guns and the marching.

The main building at Peekskill Academy. Frank was not happy there. He left after two years.

Frank stayed at Peekskill
for two long years.
Then something happened.
No one knows just what.
Maybe Frank had a heart attack.
Maybe he just fainted.

But Frank's parents let him
come home at last.

For his fourteenth birthday,
Frank's father gave him
a little printing press.
It was the perfect gift.

Frank and his brother
Harry published
newspapers (right) and
a magazine for
stamp collectors
(below right).

Frank and his
brother Harry
started a newspaper
for their neighborhood.
Then, when Frank
was seventeen,
he started another
paper and a
magazine for stamp
collectors.

Later, Frank raised fancy chickens
with his father and Harry.
So he started a magazine
about raising chickens.

Frank at age 21 (above).
He acted the part of
a young artist (left)
in a play called
The Maid of Arran.

As time passed, Frank went
from one job to another.
He was an actor for a while.
Then he began to write a musical.

Maud Gage Baum in 1900

Frank was
still working
on the musical
when he met
Maud Gage.
Soon he wanted
to marry her.

Maud's mother said Maud
would be "a darned fool"
to marry Frank.
Maud decided to be
"a darned fool."
They were married in 1882.

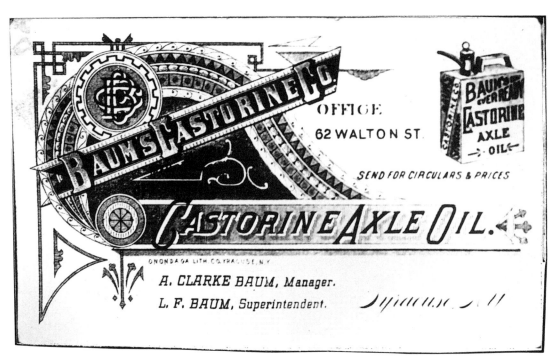

This ad is for the Castorine Axle Oil that Frank sold in the 1880s.

For a while, Frank acted
in his musical and
he and Maud traveled.
Then they rented a house in
Syracuse and Frank sold
axle grease for wagon wheels.

In 1883, Frank, Jr., was born.
Robert came along in 1886.
Now Frank was a family man.

Top left: Frank opened a store in this building in Aberdeen, South Dakota. Top right: Frank Baum in the 1890s. Below: Frank acted in plays with this theater group in Aberdeen.

Chapter 3

Oz!

The next few years brought
more moves and changes.
First the Baums moved to
Aberdeen, South Dakota,
and opened a store.

When the store
closed, Frank ran
a newspaper.
Two more little
boys, Harry and
Kenneth,
were born.

Frank's sons Kenneth (left)
and Harry. Frank had
many costumes and wigs
that the boys used
when they played "actor."

State Street in Chicago, Illinois, looked like this in the early 1890s.

In the living room of the Baums' house in Chicago: (left to right)
Frank, Jr., Robert, Harry (holding the cat), Kenneth, and Frank

At last, the Baums moved
to Chicago and Frank found
a job selling dishes.
But when he wasn't working,
he loved to tell stories
to his boys and their friends.

Sometimes Frank made up
stories about the characters
in nursery rhymes.
Maud's mother thought
those stories were good.

She made Frank send
them to a publisher.
Mother Goose in Prose
came out in 1897.

Then Frank's heart began
to bother him again.
His doctor said he shouldn't
sell dishes anymore.
So Frank wrote full-time.

William Denslow at work on his drawings

Frank had a whole stack of
funny poems he had written.
He showed them to
an artist, William Denslow.

Denslow drew pictures
to go with the poems,
and *Father Goose, His Book,*
came out in 1899.

Till then, most pictures
in children's books were
in black and white.
But Frank and Denslow
wanted color on every page.

That was a good idea.
Father Goose became the
best-selling children's book
of the year.

One day, Frank was telling
a story to his boys
and their friends.
It was about a girl who
is blown by a cyclone
to a magic land.

All at once, something
clicked in Frank's mind.
He shooed the children away
and began to write
as fast as he could.

25

The Wonderful Wizard of Oz was Frank Baum's most famous story.

The story was about
Dorothy and her dog, Toto,
who traveled to the land of Oz.
They had adventures with
the Scarecrow, the Tin Woodsman,
and the Cowardly Lion.

Denslow painted pictures
with plenty of color,
and in 1900, *The Wonderful
Wizard of Oz* came out.

"Where did you get the name 'Oz'?"
people asked Frank.

He said he was looking
at his file drawers.
The first was labeled A-G.
The second said H-N.
The third said O-Z and
that's where he got the name.

Frank's sense of humor is shown in this portrait photo.

That *might* be true.
Or it might be another story
that Frank made up.
Sometimes he couldn't stop himself.

Frank didn't want to put
scary things in his story,
and he didn't think he had.
But some children thought
the cyclone and the Wicked Witch
of the West were pretty scary.

They didn't mind, though.
They loved the book.
The Wonderful Wizard of Oz
was the best-selling
children's book for 1900.

The Scarecrow and the Tin Woodsman from *The Wizard of Oz,*
as they looked in a stage production of the early 1900s

Chapter 4

More Oz

Soon Frank and Denslow
began work on a musical
of *The Wizard of Oz.*
Paul Tietjens wrote the music.

Paul Tietjens
wrote the music
for the stage
musical of
The Wizard of Oz.

A poster advertises the stage show *The Wizard of Oz.*

The three men worked
at Frank's house.
They sang, danced,
and acted silly.
The musical was good,
though, and did well.

That was fine
with Frank's readers.
But they really wanted
more books about Oz.
And Frank wouldn't write them.

He thought he'd told
the whole story of Oz.
So he wrote books about
other magic lands.
He even wrote a book
about Santa Claus.

But, at last, Frank
gave in and wrote
The Marvelous Land of Oz.

In *The Marvelous Land of Oz*, the Woggle-Bug and his friends (left) are prisoners in a palace. They bring materials to the roof so they can build a flying machine to escape. Below, the Woggle-Bug sits down on the grass to tell his story.

Some characters from the first book are in it. So is a wonderful new character, the Woggle-Bug. It's a people-sized insect.

John Neill drew
the pictures for
thirteen of Baum's
fourteen Oz books.

Frank and Denslow had
a fight about money.
So John Neill drew the
pictures for the new book.
he ended up doing the art
for thirteen Oz books in all.

Frank wrote other books too.
Some weren't very good.
But they earned money and
Frank always needed money.

The boys were
grown up, so
Frank and Maud
could travel—
and they did.
In 1906, they went
to Europe and
northern Africa.

But Frank still couldn't
stop writing Oz books,
even when he wanted to.
Almost every year,
he wrote a new one.

And still his readers cried,
"More!"

Chapter 5

Ozcot

In 1911, Frank and Maud
built a house
in Hollywood, California.
Frank called it Ozcot.

Ozcot was big and comfortable.
Outside were a huge birdcage,
a chicken yard, goldfish ponds,
and a beautiful garden.

Frank (above) in the
rose garden at
Ozcot with Maud
and her sister Julia.
Frank loved to
work in the Ozcot
garden (right)

Frank loved that garden.
There he dug and planted.
He wrote books there too.
Sometimes children visited
him in his garden and
Frank told them stories.

Frank liked to tell his Oz stories
to the children who visited him.

Frank and Maud surrounded by their family on Thanksgiving Day, 1918

But as time went by,
Frank's health grew worse.
He had to have an operation.
That made his heart weaker.
Soon he had to stay in bed.

On May 5, 1919,
Frank Baum had a stroke.
It took away most of
his power to speak.

But on May 6, he opened
his eyes for just a moment.
"Now we can cross
the Shifting Sands," he said.
Then, quietly, he died.

The cast of the 1939 film *The Wizard of Oz*: Dorothy,
the Cowardly Lion, the Tin Woodsman, and the Scarecrow

Twenty years after Frank died,
MGM brought out its film,
The Wizard of Oz.
Frank would have loved it.

The Wizard of Oz is one of the best-loved children's films of all time.

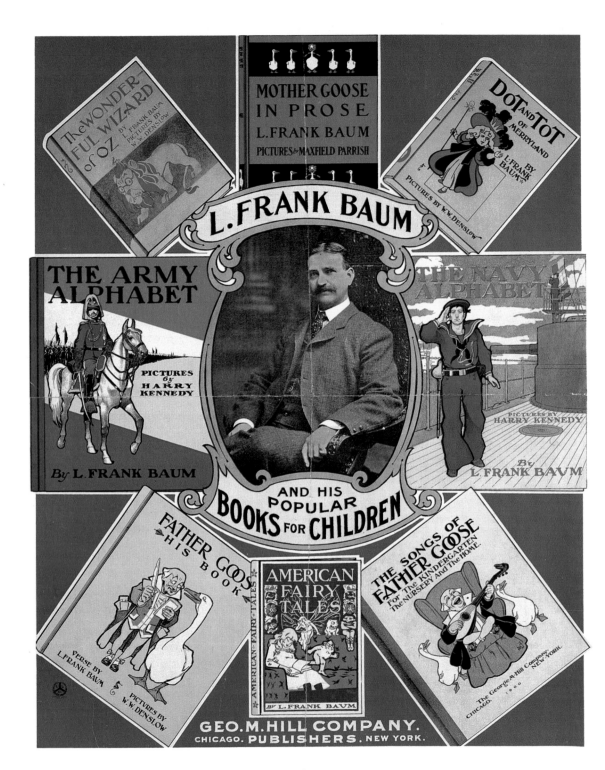

L. Frank Baum
in 1914

Today, some adults say
the Oz books are no good.
But children know better
and Frank wrote for *them*.

"I would much rather be
your story-teller," he wrote
to his young readers,
"... than to be the President."

Important Dates

1856   May 15—Born in Chittenango, New York, to Cynthia and Benjamin Baum

1868   Went to Peekskill Academy, Peekskill, New York

1870   Returned home

1882   Married Maud Gage

1888   Moved to Aberdeen, South Dakota

1891   Moved to Chicago, Illinois

1897   *Mother Goose in Prose* published

1899   *Father Goose, His Book*, published

1900   *The Wonderful Wizard of Oz* published

1911   Moved to Hollywood, California

1919   May 6—Died at Ozcot, Hollywood, California

INDEX

Page numbers in boldface type indicate illustrations.

Aberdeen, South Dakota, **18**, 19
actor, 15, **15**, 17, **18**
Baum, Benjamin, **8**
Baum, Cynthia, **8**
Baum, Frank, Jr., 17, **21**
Baum, Harry (brother), 14, **36**
Baum, Harry (son), 19, **19**, **21**
Baum, Kenneth, 19, **19**, **21**
Baum, Maud Gage (wife), 16, **16**, 17,
    22, 36, **36**, 37, **38**, 40
Baum, Robert, 17, **21**
brothers and sisters, 7
Chicago, **20**, 21, **21**
Cowardly Lion, 26, **42**, **43**
death of L. Frank Baum, 41
Denslow, William, 23, **23**, 24, 27, 31,
    35
Dorothy, 26, **42**, **43**
fairy tales, 6, 9
Father Goose, His Book, 23, 24
garden, 37, 38, **38**
heart problems, 6, 22, 40
Hollywood, California, 37
Marvelous Land of Oz, The, 33, **34**
Mother Goose in Prose, 22

musicals, 15, 17, 31, 32
Neill, John, 35, **35**
Oz, 26, 27, 33
Oz books, 33, 34, 35, 36, 45
Ozcot, 37, **37**, **38**
parents, 6, 8, 13, 14
Peekskill Academy, **10**, 11-13, **12**, **13**
pictures of L. Frank Baum, **2**, **15**, **18**,
    21, **25**, **28**, **36**, **38**, **39**, **40**, **44**, **45**
printing press, 13-14, **14**
Rose Lawn, 7, 8
Scarecrow, 26, **30**, **42**, **43**
scary things, 5-6, 9, 29
school, 8, 11
stories, 9, 21, 22, 24, 38
Syracuse, New York, 7, **7**, 17
Tietjens, Paul, 31, **31**
Tin Woodsman, 26, **30**, **42**, **43**
Toto, 26
traveling, 17, 36
Wicked Witch of the West, 29
Wizard of Oz, The, (film), 42, **42**, **43**
Woggle-Bug, 34, **34**
Wonderful Wizard of Oz, The, **26**, 27,
    29, **30**, 31, **32**

PHOTO CREDITS

ABOUT THE AUTHOR

Carol Greene has degrees in English literature and musicology. She has worked in international exchange programs, as an editor, and as a teacher of writing. She now lives in Webster Groves, Missouri, and writes full-time. She has published more than 100 books, including those in the Childrens Press Rookie Biographies series.

ABOUT THE ILLUSTRATOR

Of Cajun origins, Steven Gaston Dobson was born and raised in New Orleans, Louisiana. He attended art school in the city and worked as a newspaper artist on the *New Orleans Item*. After serving in the Air Force during World War II, he attended the Chicago Academy of Fine Arts in Chicago, Illinois. Before switching to commercial illustration, Mr. Dobson won the Grand Prix in portrait painting from the Palette and Chisel Club. In addition to his commercial work, Steven taught illustration at the Chicago Academy of Fine Arts and night school classes at LaGrange High School. In 1987, he moved to Englewood, Florida, where he says "I am doing something that I have wanted to do all of my 'art life,' painting interesting and historic people."